To the memory
of my mother

It is early in the morning. The tide is coming in. Zolani dresses quickly and runs outside. He hurries down to the rock pools and gathers mussels in a wet sack.

OVER THE GREEN HILLS

by Rachel Isadora

RED FOX

AUTHOR'S NOTE

The story takes place in the Transkei, on the east coast of South Africa.
Mpame is a village in the Transkei on the Indian Ocean.
A rondavel is a round house made of mud bricks.
It has a thatched roof. Mielies are ears of corn.

A Red Fox Book

Published by Random House Children's Books
20 Vauxhall Bridge Road, London SW1V 2SA.

A division of Random House UK Ltd
London Melbourne Sydney Auckland
Johannesburg and agencies throughout the world

Copyright © 1992 Rachel Isadora Turner

1 3 5 7 9 10 8 6 4 2

First published in the USA 1992
by Greenwillow Books

First published in Great Britain 1993
by Julia MacRae

Red Fox edition 1995

Printed in China

RANDOM HOUSE UK Limited Reg. No. 954009

ISBN 0 09 926541 9

One of their goats has wandered up to their rondavel.
Zolani puts the sack of mussels on its back.
"You don't think that fat, lazy goat will walk all the
way to Grandma Zindzi's," says Zolani's mother.
Zolani laughs and climbs down to the shore where
their other goats are grazing.

Zolani chooses a strong, young goat. He ties
the sack of mussels on its back. His mother,
with Noma settled comfortably behind her,
a box of dried fish balanced on her head, and
a basket of mielies hanging from her arm,
leads the way.

Zolani stops for a moment and looks back. The sound of the ocean seems far away. His father, he knows, is already fishing in the bay near Mpame. "I can't wait to see Grandma Zindzi," Zolani calls, and follows his mother.

They pass through the village. There are always friends outside the store, talking or waiting around. "Good morning," says Mrs. Kekana. "Where are you going?"

Onion
MANGO
GUAVA
Paw Paw

"To Grandma Zindzi's," replies Zolani's mother. "It is a long way, but what a fine day it is," says Mrs. Kekana. She gives Zolani's mother a pumpkin to take to Grandma Zindzi. Zolani's friend Gabu waves goodbye as they walk on.

The road is flecked with light. A man selling
firewood rides by. "Good day," says Zolani's
mother. "Will you trade a bundle of wood for
some dried fish?"
"Why, certainly," he says.

Two monkeys sit quietly watching. When they smell the fish, they jump up and down and swing from vine to vine.

At the edge of the forest there is a man bending over a large hole. "The heavy rains have made many holes in the road," the man tells them. "My pig is stuck, and I can't get her out. She is very heavy."

Zolani helps the man lift the pig out of the hole. The piglets nestle close to their mother. She nudges them away, and they all follow the man down the road.

"We must hurry along, too," says Zolani's mother.

They walk past fields of aloes, past farms, and over the green hills. Zolani remembers when the hills were dry and brown, when there had been no rain for a very long time. It was then that Grandma Zindzi came to live with them.

In the evenings she played her pennywhistle as they sat around the fire. One day she whittled a reed and made Zolani his own pennywhistle. She taught him to play many songs.

They stop to rest by the side of the road.
Zolani's mother feeds Noma and shares
a mango with Zolani. "Look, there is an
ostrich!" she says.

Zolani has never seen one. He runs to get
a closer look, but the ostrich speeds away.
"They are the largest birds, but they cannot
fly," says Zolani's mother.
"But they can run very fast," says Zolani,
out of breath.

A girl runs over from a roadside rondavel.
"We are selling chickens," she says.
Zolani's mother buys a speckled hen for
Grandma Zindzi. She sets it on top of the
pumpkin. It clucks a few times, then
settles down.

The road winds up a hill. On the other side is the home of Mr. and Mrs. Tombi. Zolani and his mother stop to say hello. "We have a book for you to bring to Grandma Zindzi," Mrs. Tombi says. "There are never enough books here for those who love to read. And here is a book for you, Zolani. We know you like animal stories," she adds.
Zolani is already reading as they say goodbye.
It is the first book he has ever owned.

The sun is high overhead when they reach
the village where Grandma Zindzi lives.
Zolani sees her pink rondavel, but Dolo, her
dog, does not run to greet them.
"Grandma Zindzi is not home," says Zolani.
They look all around.

"She must be visiting friends," says Zolani's mother.
They sit and wait. Zolani's mother feeds Noma.
Zolani plays his pennywhistle.
Grandma Zindzi's pet mongoose stops to listen.
Zolani picks him up carefully. "He must like
Grandma's music," he says.

Zolani is thirsty. He searches for ripe prickly pears in a nearby patch. The fruit is sweet. He picks some for his mother and Grandma Zindzi. A chameleon hides in the shade and watches for insects.

They wait and wait. It is getting late.
"I don't think Grandma Zindzi will return
today. Sometimes she visits her friends for
many days," Zolani's mother says sadly.

She ties Noma to her back, puts the box of dried
fish on top of her head, then the pumpkin,
and last of all the chicken. Then she picks up
the basket of mielies.
Zolani looks down the road, but it is empty.

The shadows are long when they leave.
Zolani looks down the road one last time.
As they walk through the village, Zolani
hears the sound of a pennywhistle.
He turns around, and there in the distance
are Grandma Zindzi and Dolo.
He runs to meet her.
"What a wonderful surprise," she says.

After dinner Zolani and Grandma sit by the fire. They look across the green hills of the Transkei. Zolani's mother is in the rondavel putting Noma to sleep. All is quiet. Grandma Zindzi and Zolani take out their pennywhistles and play their favourite songs.